CHARGE OF THE THREE-HORNED MONSTER

DINOSAUR COVE

DINOSAUR COVE™

CHARGE OF THE
THREE-HORNED MONSTER

by
REX STONE

illustrated by
MIKE SPOOR

Series created by
Working Partners Ltd

OXFORD
UNIVERSITY PRESS

For Jamie Heywood and Tom Vogler who have always loved dinosaurs.

Special thanks to Jan Burchett and Sara Vogler

OXFORD
UNIVERSITY PRESS

Great Clarendon Street, Oxford OX2 6DP
Oxford University Press is a department of the University of Oxford.
It furthers the University's objective of excellence in research, scholarship,
and education by publishing worldwide in

Oxford   New York

Auckland   Cape Town   Dar es Salaam   Hong Kong   Karachi
Kuala Lumpur   Madrid   Melbourne   Mexico City   Nairobi
New Delhi   Shanghai   Taipei   Toronto

With offices in

Argentina   Austria   Brazil   Chile   Czech Republic   France   Greece
Guatemala   Hungary   Italy   Japan   Poland   Portugal   Singapore
South Korea   Switzerland   Thailand   Turkey   Ukraine   Vietnam

Oxford is a registered trade mark of Oxford University Press
in the UK and in certain other countries

© Working Partners Limited 2008
Illustrations © Mike Spoor 2008
Eye logo © Dominic Harman 2008

Series created by Working Partners Ltd

The moral rights of the author have been asserted

Database right Oxford University Press (maker)

First published 2008

British Library Cataloguing in Publication Data

Data available

ISBN: 978-0-19-272093-1

3 5 7 9 10 8 6 4

Printed in Great Britain

Paper used in the production of this book is a natural,
recyclable product made from wood grown in sustainable forests.
The manufacturing process conforms to the environmental
regulations of the country of origin.

FACT FILE

⟹ JAMIE HAS JUST MOVED FROM THE CITY TO LIVE IN THE LIGHTHOUSE IN DINOSAUR COVE. JAMIE'S DAD IS OPENING A DINOSAUR MUSEUM ON THE BOTTOM FLOOR OF THE LIGHTHOUSE. WHEN JAMIE GOES HUNTING FOR FOSSILS IN THE CRUMBLING CLIFFS ON THE BEACH HE MEETS A LOCAL BOY, TOM, AND THE TWO DISCOVER AN AMAZING SECRET: A WORLD WITH REAL, LIVE DINOSAURS! BUT IT'S NOT ONLY DINOSAURS THAT INHABIT THIS PREHISTORIC WORLD...

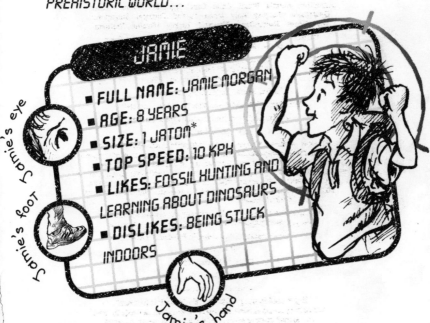

JAMIE

- **FULL NAME:** JAMIE MORGAN
- **AGE:** 8 YEARS
- **SIZE:** 1 JATOM*
- **TOP SPEED:** 10 KPH
- **LIKES:** FOSSIL HUNTING AND LEARNING ABOUT DINOSAURS
- **DISLIKES:** BEING STUCK INDOORS

Jamie's eye

Jamie's foot

Jamie's hand

*NOTE: A JATOM IS THE SIZE OF JAMIE OR TOM: 125 CM TALL AND 27 KG IN WEIGHT

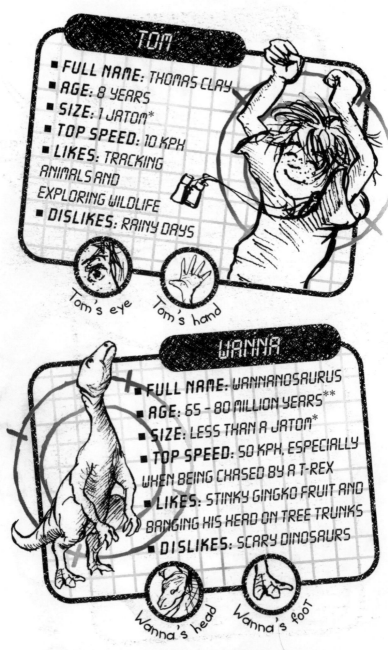

TOM

- **FULL NAME:** THOMAS CLAY
- **AGE:** 8 YEARS
- **SIZE:** 1 JATOM*
- **TOP SPEED:** 10 KPH
- **LIKES:** TRACKING ANIMALS AND EXPLORING WILDLIFE
- **DISLIKES:** RAINY DAYS

Tom's eye   Tom's hand

WANNA

- **FULL NAME:** WANNANOSAURUS
- **AGE:** 65 – 80 MILLION YEARS**
- **SIZE:** LESS THAN A JATOM*
- **TOP SPEED:** 50 KPH, ESPECIALLY WHEN BEING CHASED BY A T-REX
- **LIKES:** STINKY GINGKO FRUIT AND BANGING HIS HEAD ON TREE TRUNKS
- **DISLIKES:** SCARY DINOSAURS

Wanna's head   Wanna's foot

*NOTE: A JATOM IS THE SIZE OF JAMIE OR TOM: 125 CM TALL AND 27 KG IN WEIGHT
**NOTE: SCIENTISTS CALL THIS PERIOD THE LATE CRETACEOUS

TRICERATOPS

Triceratops's frill

Triceratops's foot

Triceratops's mouth

Triceratops's horns

- **FULL NAME:** TRICERATOPS
- **AGE:** 65 – 80 MILLION YEARS **
- **HEIGHT:** 2 JATOMS *
- **LENGTH:** 6 JATOMS *
- **WEIGHT:** 280 JATOMS *
- **HORNS:** LENGTH OF A BROOM HANDLE
- **TOP SPEED:** NORMALLY SLOW. BUT UP TO 48 KPH WHEN CHARGING
- **LIKES:** BEING ONE OF THE HERD
- **DISLIKES:** BECOMING EXTINCT. IT WAS ONE OF THE LAST TO GO

*NOTE: A JATOM IS THE SIZE OF JAMIE OR TOM: 125 CM TALL AND 27 KG IN WEIGHT
**NOTE: SCIENTISTS CALL THIS PERIOD THE LATE CRETACEOUS

DINOSAUR COVE

Village

Marina

Sealight Head

8

Landslips where clay and fossils are

DINO CAVE

Muddy beach

High Tide beach line

Sea

Smuggler's Point

Jamie Morgan sprinted along the pebbly beach of Dinosaur Cove to meet his new best friend.

'Have you got everything?' asked Tom Clay, jumping off the rock he was standing on. 'I brought my binoculars and my compass.'

Jamie took off his backpack and rummaged inside for his fossil hunting equipment. 'I've got my pocket knife, my notebook, and the Fossil Finder.' Jamie's brand new hand-held computer had all sorts of prehistoric

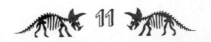

information at the touch of a few buttons.

'I brought some sandwiches, too,' Jamie said. 'Cheese and Grandad's home-made pickle. It'll blow your head off!'

'I can't wait to get back to our cave,' Tom said, hopping from one foot to another.

'You mean you can't wait to get back to the dinosaurs!' Jamie said, as the two friends hurried down the beach. Jamie had met Tom for the first time yesterday and together they had discovered Dinosaur Cove's biggest secret: an amazing world of living dinosaurs! First, Jamie had found a set of fossilized dinosaur footprints, and then the footprints had transported them to a place where dinosaurs still roamed the earth.

'It's hard keeping something so big a secret,' Tom confessed. 'My big brother kept asking me what I did yesterday.'

'I know!' Jamie replied. 'My dad got a huge triceratops skull fossil for the museum this morning, and I kept thinking about the *real* triceratops we saw yesterday.'

Jamie and his dad had moved in with his grandad to the old lighthouse on the cliffs and Jamie's dad planned to open a dinosaur museum on the ground floor. Jamie's dad knew more about dinosaurs than anyone, but he didn't know the colours of a T-Rex like Jamie and Tom did!

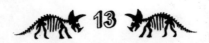

'I forgot to tell you!' panted Jamie, as they scrambled up the steep path towards their secret cave. 'I brought some coloured pencils with me. I thought we could make a map of Dino World in my notebook.'

'Good idea,' Tom said. 'We'll be like real explorers, charting unknown territories!'

'And seeing lots of dinosaurs!'

They reached the tall stack of boulders that led to their secret cave, and climbed up using cracks in the rock. From the

top of the boulders, Jamie could see his grandad fishing for lobster out in the cove.

Jamie quickly slipped into the dark cave, but Tom paused at the hidden entrance. 'What if Dino World's not there?' he asked. 'What if we dreamt it?'

Jamie laughed, and the sound echoed around the cave. 'No way! That T-Rex we met was definitely real!' With a shiver of excitement he turned on his torch and shone it into the far corner. The beam picked out the small gap in the cave wall.

Jamie took off his backpack and crawled through on his belly into the second chamber which was narrower and pitch dark. Jamie

and Tom suspected they were the only people ever to have been in this place.

Jamie flashed his torch over the stone floor. 'Here are the fossilized dinosaur footprints we found yesterday.'

'The best fossil anyone has ever found!' Tom said. The footprints had somehow transported the boys to Dino World.

Tom stepped into the first clover-shaped indent in the cave floor. 'Here goes!' He placed his foot carefully into each footprint, walking in the dinosaur tracks.

Jamie stuck close behind him and counted every step. 'One . . . two . . . three . . . four . . . FIVE!'

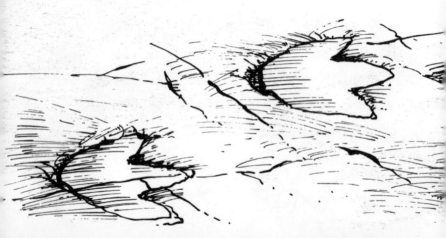

In an instant, the cold, damp cave was gone and Jamie and Tom were standing in a bright sunny cave and staring out at giant, sun-dappled trees. The air was hot and humid and they could hear the heavy drone of insects. They ran out on to the damp squelchy ground of Dino World.

'We're back in the jungle,' said Jamie happily. 'We're on Gingko Hill.'

'This is so cool!' said Tom, looking eagerly around.

Jamie laughed. 'Boiling, you mean!' He picked a large leaf off the ground and fanned himself. Suddenly he stopped. 'What was that?'

The boys listened hard. From somewhere in the steaming jungle they could hear scuffling—and it was getting nearer.

'Something's coming!' warned Tom.

Just then, a plump, scaly little creature with a flat, bony head burst out from a clump of ferns. It scuttled along on its stumpy hind legs and hurled itself at Jamie, knocking him flat on his back.

Grunk! Grunk! Grunk!

'It's Wanna!' exclaimed Tom in relief.

Jamie and Tom had met the wannanosaurus on their first visit to Dino World, and the Fossil Finder had said that it was pronounced 'wan-na-no-saur-us'. Wanna had helped them when the T-Rex was after them and turned out to be a true friend.

'Stop licking, Wanna!' panted Jamie, trying to push him off. 'Your tongue's like sandpaper.'

Tom reached up to a nearby gingko tree and picked a handful of the small, foul-smelling fruit. He held one out. 'Have a stink-o bomb, Wanna. Your favourite!'

Wanna bounded over and greedily gobbled it up as Jamie staggered to his feet. Tom gave him one more and then quickly tossed a few more pieces of the fruit to Jamie, who hid them in his backpack.

'Let's start mapping!' said Tom.

Wanna sniffed the bag as Jamie dug around and pulled out his notebook and coloured pencils. 'We're here,' he said, drawing Gingko Hill in the middle of the page. 'Yesterday we found the ocean and the lagoon in the west.' He sketched them in.

Tom checked the compass. 'So let's head north today.'

'Great,' said Jamie. 'Come on, Wanna! We're going exploring.'

Wanna wagged his tail and trotted happily alongside the boys. They scrambled through ferns and creepers and squelched among slimy giant toadstools.

At last they came to a break in the trees and peered through. Below was the dense tangle of the jungle and beyond that vast grassy plains with a wide river snaking through towards their hill.

'Look at those far away
mountains,' said Tom, scanning
the horizon with the binoculars.
'They're so high their peaks are
hidden in the clouds.'

'Far Away Mountains—that's
a good name!' said Jamie, and
scribbled it down on the map.

Then Jamie took the binoculars and scanned the plains, and what he saw made him gasp. There were about fifteen strange-looking houses made of orange earth sitting near a curve in the river.

'What is it?' Tom asked.

'I don't know,' Jamie replied. 'I think . . . I think there's a village!'

 23

'No way!' Tom said. He grabbed the binoculars and gasped. 'I thought we were the only people in Dino World.'

'Me too,' said Jamie. 'But . . . who could they be? There weren't any people around during dinosaur times. Humans didn't come along for millions of years!'

'Well, if *we're* here,' Tom reasoned, 'maybe other people got through too?'

'Or maybe the houses aren't for people at all, but something else,' Jamie guessed, as he

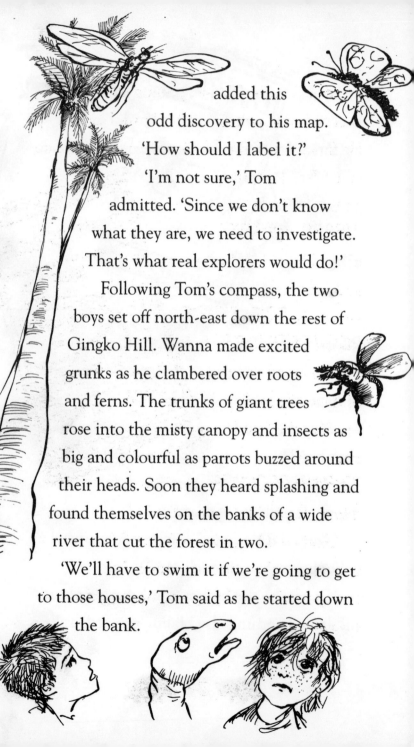

added this
odd discovery to his map.
'How should I label it?'
'I'm not sure,' Tom
admitted. 'Since we don't know
what they are, we need to investigate.
That's what real explorers would do!'
Following Tom's compass, the two
boys set off north-east down the rest of
Gingko Hill. Wanna made excited
grunks as he clambered over roots
and ferns. The trunks of giant trees
rose into the misty canopy and insects as
big and colourful as parrots buzzed around
their heads. Soon they heard splashing and
found themselves on the banks of a wide
river that cut the forest in two.

'We'll have to swim it if we're going to get
to those houses,' Tom said as he started down
the bank.

'Wait!' warned Jamie, peeling off his backpack and pulling out his Fossil Finder. He flipped open the lid. On the screen a picture of a T-Rex footprint glowed and above it the words, **'HAPPY HUNTING'**. A cursor blinked at the bottom and Jamie tapped in the keywords: **PREHISTORIC RIVER CREATURES**.

'We might meet one of these,' he said, handing the Fossil Finder to Tom.

'CHAMPSOSAURUS,' read Tom. 'Hmm. Looks like a crocodile.'

'And we'd look like its dinner!' Jamie peered into the water for signs of life and spotted several greyish humps. 'Look over there.'

'Those
are stones, fossil-
brain,' Tom said. 'We can
cross there!'

When the three of them reached
the other side, Tom checked his
compass again and they headed off
through the trees.

'How long do you think it'll take us to get
to the houses?' Tom asked.

28

'Hard to tell,' puffed Jamie. 'But we've got to figure out what those things are for our map.'

The boys stumbled into a large clearing surrounded by three walls of creepers. Spiky

plants grew all over the ground, and Wanna grabbed a clump in his mouth and chomped happily.

'OK, Wanna. Lunchtime!' declared Jamie. He climbed onto a log and tore the tinfoil off the cheese and pickle sandwiches. He was just handing a sandwich to Tom when Wanna leapt up and grabbed half of it in his mouth.

'Hey, that's my lunch!' exclaimed Tom. Wanna chewed greedily. Suddenly, the little dinosaur blinked in surprise and began to run around in circles, shaking his head and making strange gak-gak noises.

'He's discovered Grandad's pickle!' Jamie laughed.

A deep rumbling sound from the forest made Jamie and Tom instantly stop laughing.

'Only something really big could make that noise,' murmured Tom, glancing over his shoulder. 'What if it's the T-Rex again?'

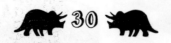

30

'Wait—I can hear mooing,' said Jamie, puzzled. His attention was fixed on the wall of creepers nearest to them.

'Like a herd of giant cows,' said Tom.

There was a sound of snapping and splitting vines. Jamie and Tom leapt to their feet as the creepers just in front of them began to shake. Jamie dropped his sandwich as the last strands tore away.

A massive beaked head with three huge horns peered into the clearing.

CHAPTER 3

'It's a triceratops!' whispered Jamie, transfixed by the giant head looming above him. 'Awesome!'

Jamie and Tom could feel its hot breath on their faces. With a snort, the dinosaur forced its body through the creepers and took a lumbering step into the clearing.

'I'm glad it's not a T-Rex,' Tom said. 'But I can't believe it's so gigantic!'

'Dad was telling me about triceratops this morning,' said Jamie. 'It weighs about five

hundred and fifty kilos—the same as an elephant!'

'I don't want that treading on my toes!' Tom hastily scrambled onto the log and pulled Jamie up behind him.

The creepers shook again and another triceratops pushed its way into the clearing. Soon a whole herd of the three-horned creatures stomped into view.

One T-tops put his head down to eat some of the spiky grass right in front of them. The herd munched on the grass, completely ignoring the boys.

'Look, Wanna!' Jamie said, as their dinosaur friend gobbled up a flower nearby. 'They're herbivores, like you, which means they won't want to eat us.'

'That's true, but if one steps on us, it would be just as dangerous!' replied Tom. 'We'd better not risk trying to walk through

them. Maybe we should try to scare them
away from the clearing?'

'I don't think scaring a herd of triceratops
would be a good idea,' Jamie said. 'They

might end up charging like a herd of elephants!'

They heard a lowing from the biggest dinosaur in the herd. The sound rumbled around the clearing as the others took up the call. It shook the boys on their log.

'The leader's given a signal,' Tom said. 'What does it mean?'

'I think it means they're moving on!' said
Jamie. 'And they're going in the direction of
the houses.'

The boys tried to keep their balance as
their log was bumped from all sides by the tree
trunk-sized legs going by, but it was too much!
Jamie slipped off the log and had to roll away
quickly to avoid being trampled.

'What are we going to do?' Jamie said,
breathlessly, as he scrambled safely back onto
the log. 'We've got to get away from their feet!'

'It seems to me that the safest place is on
top of a T-tops!' Tom said. 'Otherwise, we'll
be squished!'

'Fossil-brain!' squeaked Jamie. 'We would
need a trampoline to get up there.'

'Maybe we don't,' Tom said. He pulled some gingkoes out of Jamie's bag and held one out. One of the beasts stopped and sniffed the air. Then it turned its head to face the boys, and gave a blasting snort that nearly blew the boys off the log. Tom quickly dropped the gingko onto the ground. The beast lowered its gigantic head and its frill was in their reach. Its powerful jaws ground noisily as it chewed the orange fruit.

Tom tossed several other gingkoes onto the ground and whispered, 'Now, we can try to climb on board.'

Tom quickly took hold of the frill and pulled himself onto the triceratops's forehead, being careful not to frighten it. Then he reached down and gave Jamie a hand up. Soon they were both sitting on the leathery neck and holding on to one of the triceratops's horns.

'We're away from the huge legs, but what if it throws us off?' Jamie asked.

'I don't think it even noticed us,' Tom replied.

Their triceratops finished its gingkoes and then raised its head and began to follow the herd. Wanna stared up at them, his head on one side.

'Hey, Wanna,' waved Tom. 'Look at us!'

'This is awesome!' declared Jamie. 'It's like being on the handlebars of a giant bike.'

'Hold tight for a bumpy ride,' said Tom.

The dinosaur swayed as it plodded steadily through the tangle of jungle creepers and trees. Jamie and Tom slid about, dodging the passing branches while Wanna trotted among the legs of the herd, grunking at the top of his voice.

'This is much faster than walking!' Jamie laughed.

Suddenly the boys could see bright light through the giant leaves and branches. The herd left the jungle behind and lumbered out into the dazzling sunlight of the plains.

CHAPTER 4

Jamie squinted at the open land shimmering in the heat.

'Look!' He pointed. 'There's the river again—it comes down from the mountains.' He leaned his notebook on the triceratops's horn and drew a winding line from the mountain peaks across the plains to the jungle.

'In a way, we're the first people ever to make a map,' said Tom as the herd moved steadily across the sweltering plains.

'The first explorers, riding out on safari,' declared Jamie, laughing. 'This is great. I can see for miles!'

'Look at all these fantastic dinosaurs,' Tom said. He pointed to a slow-moving herd grazing on the leaves of some trees and spoke to an imaginary camera. 'This is Tom Clay, reporting live from Dino World, on the Great Plains. Who needs a jeep when you have the luxury of T-Tops Travel?'

Jamie laughed. He knew Tom wanted to be a famous wildlife presenter one day.

Tom went on. 'Here we are watching the alamosaurs reaching their long necks to the highest branches, and further in the distance we can see the strange dwellings that we are about to investigate. Stay tuned for what could be the most exciting discovery of all time!'

The T-tops lumbered on as the boys watched the scenery go by.

44

'Can you see that weird rock there?' said Tom, checking his compass. 'Over to the east.'

'It looks like a huge fang,' Jamie said. 'Let's call it Fang Rock!' He drew in the pointy rock and labelled it. Then he looked up. 'Hey, we're really close to the houses now.' He hurriedly put his notebook away. 'They're at least three times as tall as my dad!'

The thin towers stood in a silent group in the baking heat, silent and seemingly uninhabited.

'I don't think they are houses,' said Jamie. The mounds were made out of

bumpy orange dirt and had deep crevices running down them. There weren't any windows or doors, and Jamie couldn't imagine what kind of creature could live in them.

'There's no sign of any dinosaurs,' said Tom. 'This feels weird.'

'As if something's waiting to happen,' Jamie whispered.

The herd stopped a little way from the strange towers and mooed anxiously.

'They're signalling again,' said Tom. 'They don't seem to like the towers either.'

'I don't think Wanna understands their language,' Jamie said.

Instead of being cautious, Wanna was scrabbling excitedly at the bottom of one of the towers. All of a sudden, a stream of orange insects was pouring out of the hole and all over the little dinosaur.

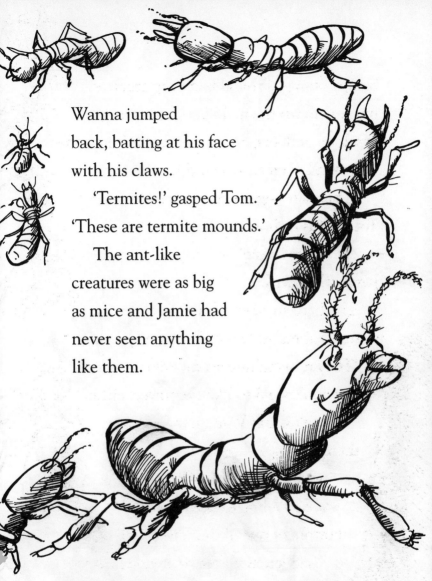

Wanna jumped
back, batting at his face
with his claws.

'Termites!' gasped Tom.
'These are termite mounds.'

The ant-like
creatures were as big
as mice and Jamie had
never seen anything
like them.

Wanna was yelping and shaking himself as
they crawled all over him.

'Wanna is too quick for them,' said Jamie, as the little dinosaur did a frantic dance. 'He's flinging them off with all that jerking around!'

'But he's scaring the triceratops!' Tom cried.

The triceratops stamped their feet in alarm and backed off, jostling each other. The shaking of the earth seemed to wake the termites and thousands of them poured out of every mound. Jamie saw the bugs stream up the legs of the leader of the herd and into its eyes and nose.

The leader tossed its head like an angry bull to shake the insects off but it was no use. It couldn't move as easily as small, agile Wanna. Suddenly it bellowed in terror and charged straight through the termite city! Dry dirt and insects scattered everywhere.

Jamie and Tom felt their T-tops lurching forward, as the other dinosaurs began to run.

'It's a stampede!' yelled Jamie. 'Hold on!'

The boys clung to the horns as the herd took off through the cloud of orange dust. Jamie felt like a rodeo rider being bucked about. Then he felt a prickle on his leg and looked down to see a termite crawling on him. Despite the bumping, Jamie managed to flick it away quickly. But soon, a whole army of termites was crawling over their T-tops's head towards him.

Jamie tried to knock away the ones that crawled onto him, but all the movement made his backpack slip from his shoulder! He flung out an arm to catch it as it fell, but it was too late. Jamie's backpack tumbled to the ground and disappeared beneath the cloud of dust.

Jamie couldn't believe it. He had lost his precious Fossil Finder and his notebook and there was nothing he could do about it.

Insects were scuttling all over him now, crawling in his hair and down his neck.

'Yow!' Jamie wailed as one termite bit him on the leg. Pain shot right down to his foot, but he managed to flick another termite away.

'I've been bitten, too!' cried Tom.

The boys tried to ignore the horrible itching and just clung on for dear life.

'Where's Wanna?' yelled Tom.

'I don't know,' Jamie shouted. 'I can't see him!'

The stampede rushed forward and all at once the herd plunged downwards.

'We're going down the riverbank!' Tom leaned back and gripped tightly as they approached the water.

Jamie gulped. 'And we're not stopping!'

SPLASH!

Their triceratops plunged into the churning river. The boys were thrown into the water among the giant thrashing dinosaurs and drowning insects. Jamie swam up to the surface and held his hands out, keeping him away from the dinosaurs' bodies and horns.

The huge dinosaurs stood in the water, seemingly relieved that the biting termites were being swept away by the river.

'They wanted to wash the termites off,' Jamie managed to splutter.

'And us too!' Tom replied. The boys felt the pull of the river and soon were sucked into the current.

'Thanks for the ride!' Jamie called out as they left their triceratops taxi far behind.

Jamie heard a grunking noise nearby. 'Wanna!' he cried. The little dinosaur was running along the riverbank trying to keep pace with them and he had something in his mouth.

'Your backpack!' Tom exclaimed. 'It's safe!'

'Go, Wanna!' shouted Jamie.

Jamie and Tom were both good swimmers but the current was too strong to let them swim to the edge. When a log swept by, Jamie and Tom grabbed on to its stubby branches.

'Phew,' gasped Tom as he got a good hold. He checked out the river ahead. 'Do you think there are any champsosaurs in here?'

'I hope not,' Jamie groaned. 'I think we've met enough prehistoric beasts for one day.'

The boys' log floated into a patch of shadow and Tom looked up. 'It's Fang Rock!' he said. 'We must be going towards Gingko Hill—and home!'

'Maybe it will take us all the way back, and save us the walk.' Jamie grinned.

The river twisted round Fang Rock and out again into the sunshine. They could see Wanna on the bank. He was jumping up and down and grunking excitedly.

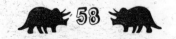

'What's the matter with Wanna?' Tom
wondered aloud.

Jamie heard the sound of rushing water,
and soon the boys' log was being knocked this
way and that between sharp rocks. The water
churned and bubbled, and Jamie realized that
he could see the river ahead of them
disappear. The land on either side of the river
fell away and Jamie realized what Wanna was
trying to warn them about. 'It's a waterfall!'

The boys kicked
frantically towards
the bank but
the current

was too strong. The log bumped and spun on towards the dangerous drop.

Just before the boys were about to go over, the log caught suddenly between two rocks. The boys only just managed to hold on as white water crashed over their shoulders.

'Phew!' exclaimed Jamie. He could just see over the fall down to a large swirling pool below and was relieved that the log had saved them. He gave Tom a wobbly smile. 'Let's get out of here.'

Creeeeak!

'What was that?' he gasped.

'The log's splitting from the force of the current!' yelled Tom. 'We're going to go over the waterfall!'

Jamie caught at his arm. 'Take a deep breath when you fall!' he shouted urgently. 'Start swimming the moment you can!'

Crack!

The log broke and the boys were sucked through the white foaming water and over the edge.

CHAPTER 6

'Aaaah!' Jamie shouted as he plummeted down and down.

He took a huge breath just in time.

SPLASH!

He hit the churning water and plunged under the surface, tumbling round and round. Jamie felt the waterfall pushing him to the bottom of the river. He opened his eyes but it was murky and dark and all he could see were

bubbles swirling around him. He couldn't even tell which way up was.

Then his foot touched rock. He pushed away hard, kicking his legs for all they were worth. At last he was at the surface, gulping in the wonderful air. He swam around, looking for Tom. He hoped his friend was all right!

Suddenly, the water beside him erupted and Tom bobbed up like a cork, gasping for breath.

Jamie and Tom looked up in awe at the huge waterfall they had just come over. 'We made it!'

'A huge waterfall, an army of termites, a ride on a triceratops,' Tom said. 'Another great adventure in Dino World!'

The boys swam away from the waterfall and let the gentle current take them downstream. Ahead the river disappeared

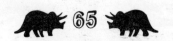

back into the jungle. The current swept them round to the right where the trees were dense and tangled with creepers.

The river now became wider and slower. With weak strokes, the boys made their way to the side and grabbed hold of an overhanging branch.

'I can touch the bottom,' gasped Tom. 'There's a ledge.'

They dragged themselves out of the water and collapsed on the safe, dry bank.

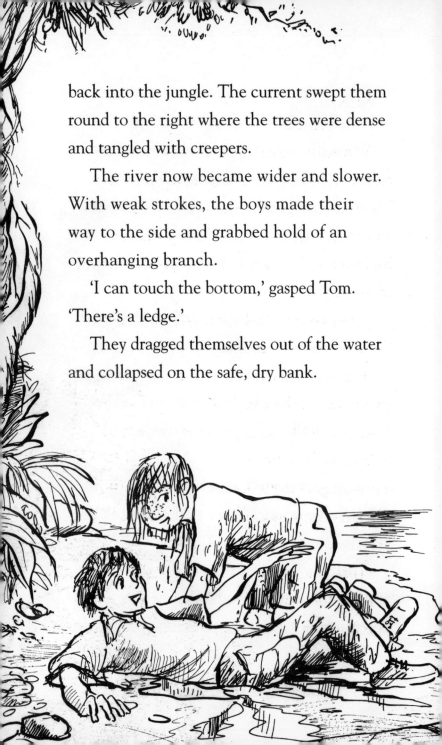

Grunk
         grunk!

Wanna bounded up and threw himself
on them, licking and nudging them in turn.
Then he disappeared into the undergrowth
and came back a moment later with the
backpack in his mouth. He dropped it in front
of the boys.

Jamie sat up. 'He kept it safe! Well done,
Wanna. You're a real mate.'

Tom reached over and got a
gingko out of the bag. 'You
deserve this!' he said, giving it
to Wanna. The little
dinosaur gobbled it down
and gave Tom another
huge lick.

'Yuck!' he cried,
pushing him away.
'Stink-o breath!'

'Where are we?' asked Jamie.

'Well, you've got the map!' laughed Tom.

Jamie pulled it out and the boys had a look around. There was a steep slope ahead of them, covered in a thick wall of trees.

'I can just hear the waterfall,' said Tom. He got to his feet and peered through the binoculars. 'Yes, it's back there. It must be— look, there's the point of Fang Rock.'

He checked his compass. 'It's east of here.'

They looked at their map.

'And the river comes from the mountains in the north-east and flows across the plains.' Jamie traced it with his finger.

'Then it goes through the jungle here— where we are,' added Tom.

Jamie gazed at the trees ahead of them. 'Then we must be at the bottom of Gingko Hill. Told you it would save us the walk!'

Tom checked his watch. 'Lucky this is waterproof,' he grinned. 'It's not long before the tide comes in. We don't want to get trapped in the cliffs.'

Jamie nodded. 'Grandad will be back with his lobsters and he'll be wondering where we are.' He picked up his backpack. 'Who'd have thought making a map would be such an adventure?'

They climbed back up Gingko Hill. As they passed the break in the trees, Jamie looked back out over the plains. He could see

69

the termite mounds in the distance, and beyond that, on the other side of the river, was the grazing triceratops herd.

'Those termite bites really hurt when we got them,' said Jamie, pulling up his trousers to reveal a purple pus-filled bump the size of an apricot. 'But they don't really hurt any more.'

'Ew!' Tom crinkled up his nose. 'That looks so gross.' Tom pulled up his T-shirt to reveal the bite on his stomach that had a greenish ring around it.

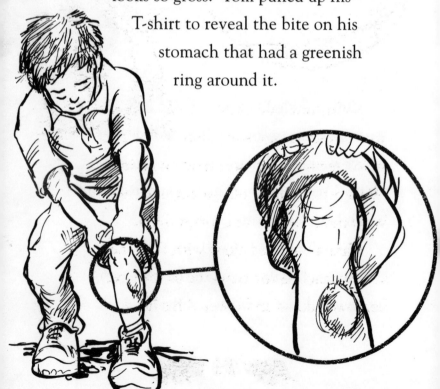

'Yours is even bigger!'
Jamie declared.

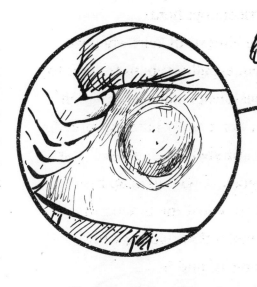

'Prehistoric bug bites.'
Tom poked the squishy bump
which seemed ready to pop at any minute.
'We'd better not let our parents see these!
We'd never be able to explain them.'

Wanna bounded along with them but
as they reached the entrance to the cave,
he slowed down and lowered his head.

Grunk?

'See you, Wanna,' said Jamie, patting him on his hard, flat head. 'We'll be back soon.'

'And that's a promise!' added Tom. He pulled out the last two gingko fruits.

Wanna wagged his tail and gobbled up his treat happily.

Jamie and Tom stepped into the cave. Jamie placed his feet in the dinosaur

footprints and felt the ground get harder as he went. On his fifth step, he was plunged into inky darkness, and he was back in the cave in Dinosaur Cove. A moment later, Tom was standing next to him.

Jamie flicked on his torch and led the way out of the cave, down the rock fall, and back along the path to the beach.

'What an adventure!' said Tom.

'Better than any theme park,' agreed Jamie. He fished out his notebook and flicked to the map. 'Look how far we travelled today! Right out on to the plains—and back the quick way!' He pointed to Fang Rock. 'The waterfall was just here. What shall we call it?'

'Crashing Rock Falls!' declared Tom.

'Cool! Maybe I'll draw us going over the edge.' Jamie grinned.

'Ahoy there, boys!' Grandad was rowing back towards the beach.

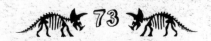

The boys waved and ran down to the sea.

'Come on,' he called. 'I can't land the boat without your help.'

Jamie and Tom jumped into the surf and waded out to the boat, helping Grandad pull the boat up the beach.

'The moment we're done, Jamie,' Grandad said as they unloaded the full lobster pots,

'you must show Tom the new triceratops skull.
It's sixty-five million years old.' He clapped
Tom on the back. 'I bet you haven't seen
anything like that before!'

Jamie and Tom smiled at each other.
Grandad would never believe what they *had*
seen today in Dino World!

DINOSAUR WORLD

- - - - - BOYS' ROUTE

Jung[...]

Misty
Lagoon

White
Ocean

76

Far Away Mountains

Crashing Rock Falls

Great Plains

Fang Rock

Gingko Hill

GLOSSARY

Alamosaurus (al-am-oh-sor-us) – a gigantic dinosaur with a vegetarian diet that searched for food with its long neck and tiny head while protecting itself with its long, whip-like tail.

Champsosaurus (champ-so-sor-us) – crocodile-like prehistoric creature with a long, thin, tooth-filled snout, living and hunting in rivers and swamps.

Fossil – the remains or imprint of plants or animals found in rocks. They help scientists unravel the mysteries of prehistoric times.

Fossil Finder – hand-held computer filled with dinosaur facts.

Gingko (gink-oh) – a tree native to China called a 'living fossil' because fossils of it have been found dating back millions of years, yet they are still around today. Also known as the stink-bomb tree because of its smelly apricot-like fruit.

Herbivore – an animal that only eats plants; a vegetarian.

Termite – ant-like insects that grow as big as mice in Dino World. These prehistoric pests lived and worked together to build orange house-high mounds out of soil and spit, and there are still several kinds of termites around today.

Triceratops (T-tops) (try-serra-tops) – a three-horned, plant-eating dinosaur which looks like a rhinoceros.

Tyrannosaurus Rex (T-Rex) (ti-ran-oh-sor-us rex) – a meat-eating dinosaur with a huge tail, two strong legs but two tiny arms. T-Rex was one of the biggest and scariest dinosaurs.

Wannanosaurus (wah-nan-oh-sor-us) – a dinosaur that only ate plants and used its hard, flat skull to defend itself. Named after the place it was discovered: Wannano in China.

Get ready!
I'm next ...